# ERIC CARLE
# CLASSICS

Eric Carle
CLASSICS

Simon & Schuster Books for Young Readers

NEW YORK   LONDON   TORONTO   SYDNEY

# ERIC CARLE
# CLASSICS

## The Tiny Seed

## Pancakes, Pancakes!

## Walter the Baker

# The Tiny
# Seed

It is Autumn.

A strong wind is blowing. It blows flower seeds high in the air and carries them far across the land. One of the seeds is tiny, smaller than any of the others. Will it be able to keep up with the others? And where are they all going?

One of the seeds flies higher than the others. Up, up it goes! It flies too high and the sun's hot rays burn it up. But the tiny seed sails on with the others.

Another seed lands on a tall and icy mountain.
The ice never melts, and the seed cannot grow.
The rest of the seeds fly on. But the tiny seed
does not go as fast as the others.

Now they fly over the ocean. One seed falls into the water and drowns. The others sail on with the wind. But the tiny seed does not go as high as the others.

One seed drifts down onto the desert. It is hot and dry, and the seed cannot grow. Now the tiny seed is flying very low, but the wind pushes it on with the others.

Finally the wind stops and the seeds fall gently down on the ground. A bird comes by and eats one seed. The tiny seed is not eaten. It is so small that the bird does not see it.

Now it is Winter.
After their long trip the seeds settle down. They look just as if they are going to sleep in the earth. Snow falls and covers them like a soft white blanket. A hungry mouse that also lives in the ground eats a seed for his lunch. But the tiny seed lies very still and the mouse does not see it.

Now it is Spring.
After a few months the snow has melted. It is really spring!
Birds fly by. The sun shines. Rain falls. The seeds grow so
round and full they start to burst open a little.
Now they are not seeds any more. They are plants. First
they send roots down into the earth. Then their little stems
and leaves begin to grow up toward the sun and air.
There is another plant that grows much faster than the
new little plants. It is a big fat weed. And it takes all the
sunlight and the rain away from one of the small new
plants. And that little plant dies.

The tiny seed hasn't begun to grow yet. It will be too late!
Hurry! But finally it too starts to grow into a plant.

The warm weather also brings the children out to play.
They too have been waiting for the sun and spring time.
One child doesn't see the plants as he runs along and —
Oh! He breaks one! Now it cannot grow any more.

The tiny plant that grew from the tiny seed is growing fast, but its neighbor grows even faster. Before the tiny plant has three leaves the other plant has seven! And look! A bud! And now even a flower!

But what is happening? First there are footsteps. Then a shadow looms over them. Then a hand reaches down and breaks off the flower.

A boy has picked the flower to give to a friend.

It is Summer.
Now the tiny plant from the tiny seed is all alone.
It grows on and on. It doesn't stop. The sun shines
on it and the rain waters it. It has many leaves.
It grows taller and taller. It is taller than the people.
It is taller than the trees. It is taller than the houses.
And now a flower grows on it. People come from
far and near to look at this flower. It is the tallest
flower they have ever seen. It is a giant flower.

All summer long the birds and bees and butterflies come visiting. They have never seen such a big and beautiful flower.

Now it is Autumn again.
The days grow shorter. The nights grow cooler. And
the wind carries yellow and red leaves past the flower.
Some petals drop from the giant flower and they sail
along with the bright leaves over the land and down
to the ground.

The wind blows harder. The flower has lost almost all of its petals. It sways and bends away from the wind. But the wind grows stronger and shakes the flower. Once more the wind shakes the flower, and this time the flower's seed pod opens. Out come many tiny seeds that quickly sail far away on the wind.

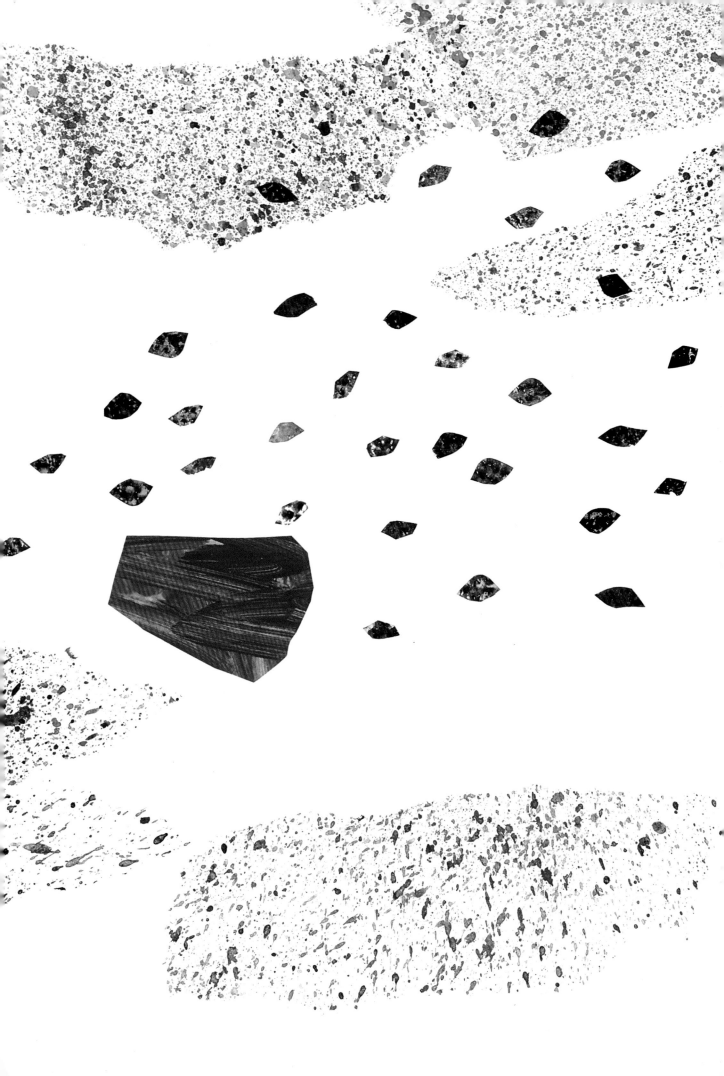

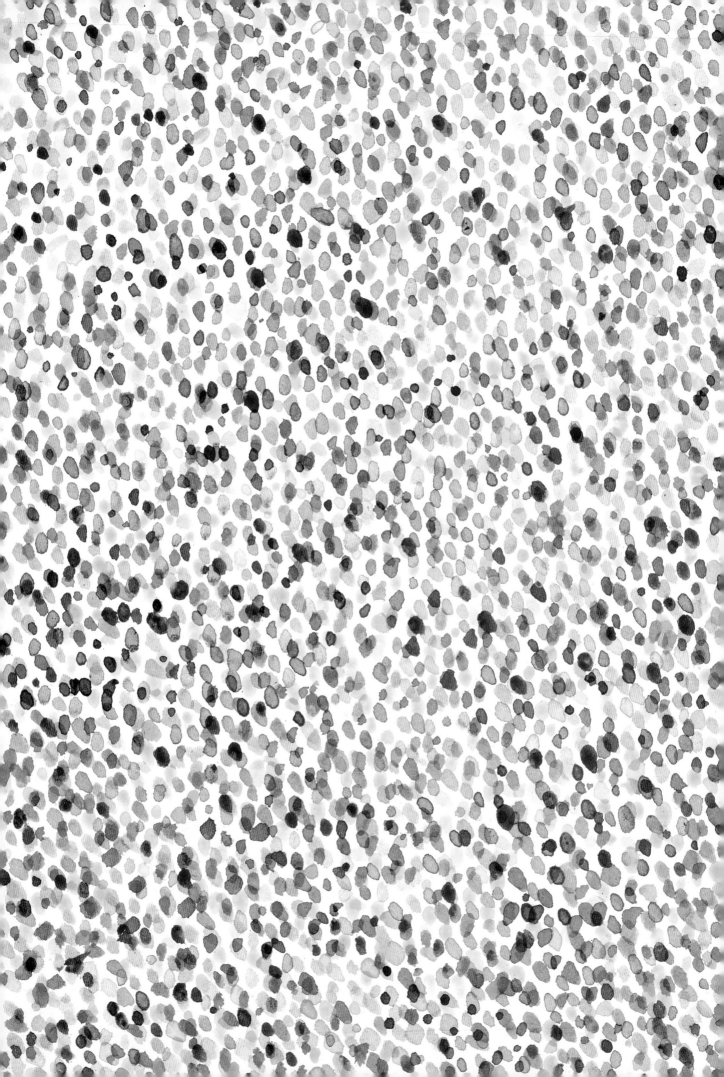

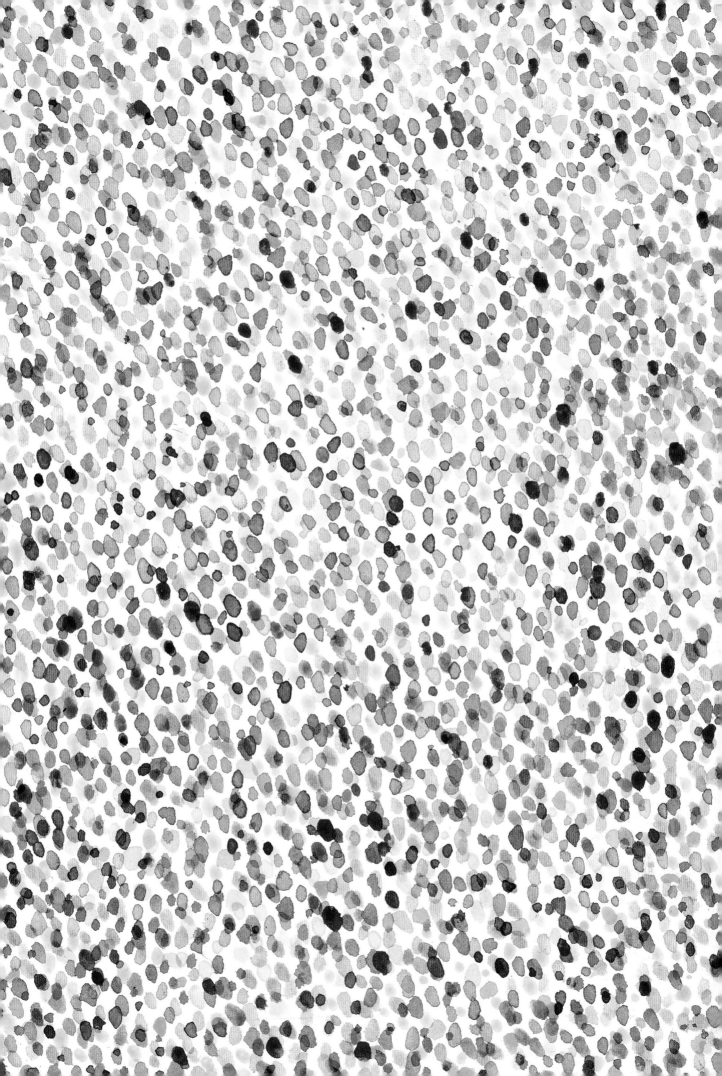

# Pancakes, Pancakes!

**Kee-ke-ri-kee**

crowed the rooster.
Jack woke up, looked out
the window and thought,
"I'd like to have a
big pancake for breakfast."

Jack's mother was already up and busy.
"Mother," said Jack, "I'd like to have a big pancake for breakfast."
"I am busy and you will have to help me," she said.
"How can I help?" asked Jack.
"We'll need some flour," she replied.

"Take a sickle and cut as much wheat as the donkey can carry.
Then take it to the mill. The miller will grind it into flour."

When Jack had cut enough wheat,
he put it on the donkey's back and took it to the miller.

"Can you grind this wheat for me?" he asked.
"I need it for a big pancake."
"First we must separate the grain from the chaff," said the miller.

He gave Jack a flail and spread the wheat onto the ground.
The miller took another flail and began to beat the wheat with it.
Jack helped with the threshing,
and soon there was a big pile of straw and chaff–
and a small pile of grain.

The miller poured the grain on a large flat stone.
On top of it was a round millstone
connected to the water wheel on the outside.
The water wheel turned round and round,
turning the millstone round and round, too,
to grind the grain into flour.
At last the miller handed Jack a bag of flour.

"Here's the flour," shouted Jack. "Let's make a pancake."
But his mother said, "Now we need an egg."
Jack went to the black hen and fed her some grain that had slipped
into his pocket while he had been threshing.
"Cluck, cluck," said the black hen and went inside the hen house.
Then she said, "Cluck, cluck," once more and laid an egg.

"Here's an egg," shouted Jack. "Let's make a pancake."
But his mother said, "Now we need some milk."
Jack went to the spotted cow and began to milk her.
"Moo, moo," said the spotted cow as the milk squirted into the pail.

"Here's the milk," shouted Jack. "Let's make a pancake."
But his mother said, "We need some butter."
Jack got the butter churn and held it between his knees.
His mother scooped the cream from the top of the milk
and put it into the butter churn.
Jack pushed the churn handle up and down, up and down.
Finally, the cream turned into butter.

"Here's the butter," shouted Jack. "Let's make a pancake."
But his mother said, "We need to build a fire."
Jack went to the woodshed and brought some firewood.

"Here's the firewood," shouted Jack. "Let's make a pancake."
But his mother said,
"Wouldn't you like to have something sweet on your pancake?"
So Jack went down to the cool cellar
and pulled a jar of strawberry jam from one of the shelves.

"Here's the strawberry jam," shouted Jack.
"Let's make a pancake."
In the kitchen, Jack's mother had filled the table with
the flour,
the egg,
the milk,
the butter.

There was also
a mixing bowl,
a cup,
a wooden spoon,
a ladle,
a frying pan,
a plate,
a knife, fork, and spoon.
And a jar of strawberry jam.

And his mother said, "Put a cupful of flour into the bowl…

"Break an egg into the flour and stir…

"Pour a cupful of milk over the flour and eggs and stir again until the batter is smooth and without lumps."

Jack's mother heated the frying pan over the fire,
and added a piece of butter. The butter melted fast.

Then she said to Jack,
"Now pour a ladleful of batter into the hot pan."

After a minute or two she looked at the underside of the pancake.
It was golden brown.
"Now watch," she said, "I'll turn the pancake over. Ready?"

"Ready!" shouted Jack.
"Flip," said his mother.
Up and over went the pancake high into the air
and landed right in the pan. In another minute or two
the pancake was crisp on the underside as well.

Then she slipped the pancake from the frying pan onto the plate
and spread some strawberry jam on it.
"And now, Jack," his mother started to say,
but Jack said...

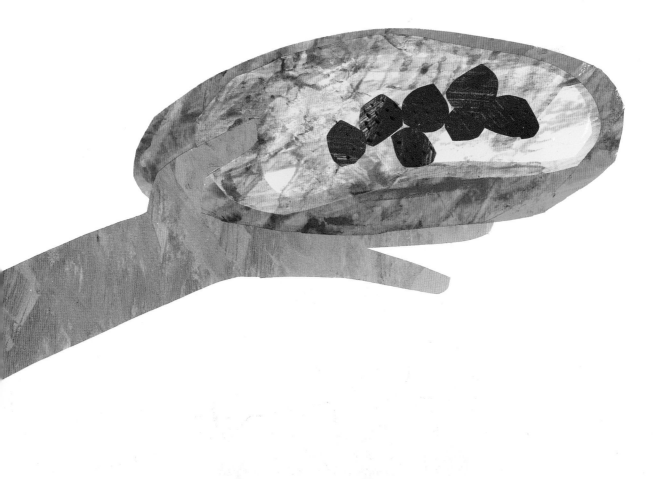

"Oh, Mama, I know what to do now!"

# Walter the Baker

Long ago, in a town encircled by a wall,
lived Walter the Baker, his wife Anna, and their son Walter Jr.

Walter the Baker was known even outside the walls of the town.
He was the best baker in the whole Duchy.
Early every morning, while everybody else was still asleep,
Walter began baking his breads, rolls, cookies, tarts, and pies.

Anna sold the baked goods in the store.
No one could resist the warm, sweet smells drifting from Walter's bakery.
People came from near and far.

The Duke and Duchess who ruled over the Duchy
loved Walter's sweet rolls.
Every morning Walter Jr. carried a basketful of warm sweet rolls
to the castle where they lived.

"Mm," said the Duchess, spreading quince jelly on her roll.
"Ahh," said the Duke, putting honey on his.
  And so each day was the same as the day before—
                                    until one early morning…

…when Walter's cat was chasing a mouse and tipped over the can of milk.
"What will I do?" cried Walter.
"I cannot make sweet rolls without fresh milk."
In desperation, Walter grabbed a pitcher of water.
"I hope nobody will notice the difference," he said
as he poured the water into the flour to make the dough.

Now, you and I may not be able to tell the difference between a roll made with water and one made with milk.
But the Duke and especially the Duchess could tell the difference.
"Ugh," cried the Duchess after she took a bite.
"What is this!" roared the Duke.
"Where is Walter the Baker? Bring him here at once!"

So Walter was brought before the Duke.

"What do you call this?" roared the Duke.

"This is not a roll, this is a stone!" And with that he threw it at Walter's feet.

"I used water instead of milk," Walter admitted, hanging his head in shame.

"Pack your things and leave this town and my Duchy forever,"
shouted the Duke. "I never want to see you again!"

"My Duke," pleaded Walter, "this is my home. Where will I go?
Please give me one more chance, please."

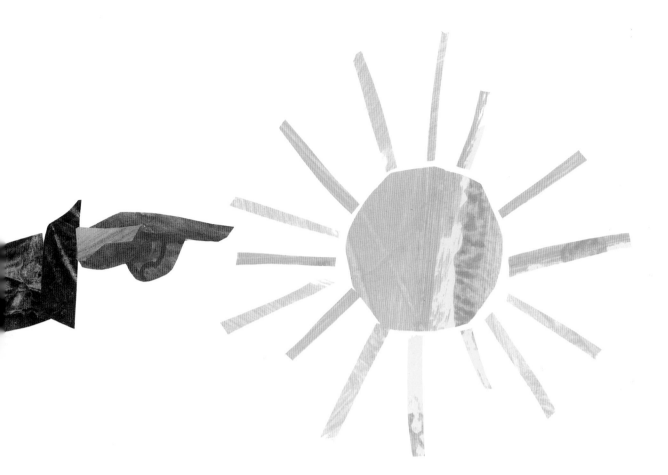

"I must banish you," said the Duke.
 But then he remembered Walter's good rolls and how much he
 and the Duchess would miss them.
"Well, Walter…" the Duke started to say.
 Then he thought and thought some more.
"You may stay if you can invent a roll through which the rising sun
 can shine three times."
 And to make it more difficult, he added, "It must be made from
 one piece of dough, and most of all, it must taste good.
 Now go home and bring me such a roll tomorrow morning."
 Poor Walter!  Worried and sad, he trudged back to his bakery.

Walter worked all day and into the night.
He made long rolls, short rolls, round rolls, twisted rolls.
He made thin rolls and he made fat rolls.
And he worked some more.

Walter beat, pulled, pushed, and pounded the dough.

But it was all in vain.

He could not come up with a roll that would please the Duke.
By early morning Walter had only one long piece of dough left.
"It's hopeless," he cried.
In a sudden fit of anger, he grabbed the last piece of dough
and flung it against the ceiling.
"Stick there!" he yelled at the dough.
But it didn't. It fell, twisting itself as it dropped down
and plopped into a pail of water.

Anna and Walter Jr. were awakened by Walter's yell and
rushed into the bakery just as Walter was about to dump out
the water and the twisted piece of dough.
"Father, stop!" shouted Walter Jr. "Look!"

And Anna quickly popped the dough into the hot oven.
Soon it was brown and crisp.
She took out the roll and handed it to Walter.
It hadn't risen very high, but it had three holes.

Walter held up the twisted roll and smiled.
He saw that the morning sun was shining through it three times.

Walter put the roll into a basket and rushed to the castle
to deliver his invention to the Duke and Duchess.
And they too saw the morning sun shine through it three times.
Then the Duke and Duchess each took a small bite.
Walter was afraid to look, because he had no idea how it would taste.
"Well done!" said the Duke.
"Perfect!" exclaimed the Duchess.
Both were glad that Walter would not have to be sent away.

And Walter too was happy that he could stay.

"Now, pray tell us, Walter. What do you call this?" asked the Duke.

"Uh, yes, pray us tell…" Walter stammered, as he tried to come up with a name.

"What was that? Pra… pre… pretzel?" said the Duke. "Pretzel it shall be. From now on," he declared, "it shall be sweet rolls in the morning…"

"… and pretzels in the afternoon," said the Duchess.

Walter returned to his bakery and spent all day and night making pretzels.
The next morning there were baskets of pretzels outside the store for
the whole town to taste.
And a special basket of pretzels for the Duke and Duchess.
And a cheer went up for Walter the Pretzel Maker.

The word pretzel comes from the Latin word bracchium, meaning "arm."
The pretzel was originally a simple bread eaten during Lent. Its shape is based
on an ancient position for prayer in which the arms were folded across
the chest and the hands were placed on opposite shoulders.

ACKNOWLEDGMENTS

For *Walter the Baker*: I wish to thank my neighbor Robert Normand, Bakery and Konditorei in Northampton, Massachusetts, for his technical assistance.

SIMON & SCHUSTER BOOKS FOR YOUNG READERS
An imprint of Simon & Schuster Children's Publishing Division
1230 Avenue of the Americas, New York, New York 10020
*Pancakes, Pancakes!* copyright © 1970, 1990 by Eric Carle Corp.
Copyright renewed © 1998 by Eric Carle Corp.
*The Tiny Seed* copyright © 1970, 1987 by Eric Carle Corp.
Copyright renewed © 1998 by Eric Carle Corp.
*Walter the Baker* copyright © 1972, 1995 by Eric Carle
Copyright renewed © 2000 by Eric Carle
These titles were previously published individually by Simon & Schuster Books for Young Readers.
Eric Carle's name and his signature logotype are trademarks of Eric Carle.
All rights reserved, including the right of reproduction in whole or in part in any form.
SIMON & SCHUSTER BOOKS FOR YOUNG READERS is a trademark of Simon & Schuster, Inc.
For information about special discounts for bulk purchases, please contact Simon & Schuster Special Sales at 1-866-506-1949 or business@simonandschuster.com.
The Simon & Schuster Speakers Bureau can bring authors to your live event. For more information or to book an event, contact the Simon & Schuster Speakers Bureau at 1-866-248-3049 or visit our website at www.simonspeakers.com.
The illustrations for this book are done in collage.
Manufactured in China
0711 SCP
10 9 8 7 6 5 4 3 2 1
CIP data for this book is available from the Library of Congress.
ISBN 978-1-4424-3988-7

## DEDICATIONS

*The Tiny Seed*

For Ann Beneduce

*Pancakes, Pancakes!*

For Clinton and Clifton

*Walter the Baker*

For my mother and father